7

THE VIDEO AVENGER

Douglas Colligan

ILLUSTRATIONS BY RAY LAGO

SCHOLASTIC INC.
New York Toronto London Auckland Sydney Tokyo

ISBN 0-590-32869-7

12 11 10 9 8 7 6 5 4 3 2 1   11   3 4 5 6 7/8

Printed in the U.S.A.   01

BEWARE!!!
DO NOT READ THIS BOOK FROM BEGINNING TO END!

You are about to step into a world completely controlled by one of the smartest computers you'll ever meet. You will compete with the machine in all kinds of games and electronic challenges. Make the right moves, and you will have a lot of fun. Guess wrong, and your game could be all over!

You will soon find out there is more than one adventure lurking in the pages of this book. The twists and turns are up to you. If you don't like the way your story is going, go back and try another route. Think twice — three times even — before you turn a page — or push a button!

There's only one way in, but there are many ways out of this book. All you have to do is outsmart the computer.

So, good luck. And may you never cross the wrong circuits!

Now turn to PAGE 2.

It's the big day. You've received word from your local Burger Bomb restaurant that you won one of the five grand giveaway prizes: a slick, super-smart MEE-II computer. And today is the day they promised to deliver it.

Sure enough, a truck pulls up in front of your house, and the driver leaves a small mountain of cardboard cartons on your front steps. Those 4,789 cheeseburgers you ate paid off!

You drag the boxes up to your room, rip open the big one marked COMPUTER, and ... uh-oh. Inside is not a MEE-II but a big black machine with silver knobs and switches and a video screen built right into the front. Was this supposed to go to that mysterious new laboratory down the street, the one with the high wire fences and armed guards? Maybe the driver delivered the wrong machine by mistake.

In no time, you have all the boxes opened and the computer hooked up. You press the button stamped START. The machine makes a soft hum, and blink — hey, there's your favorite video game: Death-Beam Dinosaurs. Just then your sister Kate bursts into the room. "Hey! You got the computer! What are we going to play on it?"

"I'm going to play Death-Beam Dinosaurs," you say, pushing her out of the room.

Go on to PAGE 4.

4

On the screen is a small, silvery spaceship and a weird, seven-headed flying dinosaur that fires death beams from each of its mouths. To score points, you have to get the spaceship to blast the head that is shooting out the beam. If you miss, you waste a valuable shot. If you blast a nonshooting head, the dinosaur splits in two, and you double your trouble. You're all ready to play, but you can't find the controls. Just then a voice comes out of the computer.

"Hello, human."

"Uh, hello," you mumble. "Who are you?"

"I am the voice of Computer Control. I will show you how to operate the machine. Are you ready to play the game?"

"Well, yes, but there are no controls," you point out.

"No problem. You see that small spaceship on the screen?"

"Yup."

"Touch it," commands Computer Control.

"What?"

"Touch your finger to the spot where the spaceship appears on the screen."

Weirdest game I ever heard of, you think. But you want to humor this thing. So you put your finger on the tiny glowing spaceship. That's when it happens.

Go on to PAGE 5.

There's a flash of light, a loud zzzzzzzzzz, and you're flying straight into the video screen. Everything is a blur at first, but finally you find yourself sitting at some sort of control panel overlooking the shimmering acres of a video landscape. Computer Control starts talking to you again, this time through the panel.

"You are now in video world. The games you play are for real, and the stakes are high. One wrong move, and you get fired into a tiny electronic blip. Good luck, human."

"Hold it," you shout. "I don't feel like playing games right now."

"Too late. You have to let the program run its course."

Then, out of the corner of your eye, you see an enormous, green, seven-headed dinosaur drifting toward your ship. You grab the control stick and ... wait a minute, what's this? There's a big, black HYPER-SPACE button among the controls. If it works like other games, one push will rocket you to someplace else. Still, it might be fun to take on the dinosaur. You don't get to play a game like this every day.

If you hit the HYPERSPACE button, turn to PAGE 11.

If you decide to take on the dinosaur, turn to PAGE 12.

You wait quietly. The dinosaur edges closer. You slowly line up your shot. Your thumb settles on top of the FIRE button, and just as the dangerous head enters your sights, you fire.

The dinosaur dives down a bit, and your shot skims by, disappearing into the black void beyond. Then one of the heads on the right fires. You barely manage to get out of the way. You sight in on it and fire. *Bam!* Perfect shot. Two heads gone. A third head gets ready to beam. You swing around and blast it into nothingness. "Four shots left," you hear your control panel tell you. Four shots. Four heads. You can't afford to waste anything this time.

Something funny is going on. The dinosaur is not moving. You watch. One head starts to move. It could be a trick. It is! You spot a different head opening its mouth. You aim and blast it away. A split second later another head shoots. You make your ship dive to safety. You swing back up, sight, and shoot. *Blap!* Another head gone.

There are only two shots left. What now? The ship is running out of power.

If you decide to fire at the head on the right, turn to PAGE 72.

If you decide to fire at the head on the left, turn to PAGE 22.

REMEMBER, if you hit the wrong head you'll have two dinosaurs to fight.

The strange-looking woman walks over to a vacant landing circle and lifts it up by the edge, like a giant trapdoor. Underneath is a tunnel. A little nervously, you step in and — surprise — there is no step! You fall down a long black hole. As light as a feather, you drift to the ground. The woman floats down next to you. Looking around, you see a group of people.

The woman whispers as you walk toward the crowd, "Be careful to whom you talk here. The computer has its spies among us."

"Where are we?"

"In a forgotten pocket of circuitry, one the computer can't reach with its power."

"Who are all these people?"

"Those who played the machine and lost," she says. "Some of them helped to build this. They wanted to make this the smartest machine ever. Unfortunately, they did just that."

"I guess that means I'm stuck here, too," you say, sighing.

"Not if you're willing to help. With you on our side, we all might be able to get out. Will you join us?"

If you decide to join them, turn to PAGE 19.

You notice an opening off to one side that you would like to try on your own. Find out where it leads on PAGE 70.

You flip a coin onto the back of your hand and then look.

"It's heads," you tell the computer.

"Ah, well, then you'll need a copilot. Zone B is extremely tricky."

Right then you see a spark, followed by a cloud of bright yellow smoke in the seat next to you. "The ship's on fire!" you holler.

"No, it's not. That's your copilot, an intelligent cluster of electrons. It knows everything there is to know about the games in here."

Doesn't look so smart, you think. "How is a ball of smoke supposed to help? It can't even talk."

"It has telepathy and can read your thoughts. Try it."

Very strange. Well, it's worth a try. "Hello, copilot," you think.

Hello, sounds a high-pitched voice in your head.

"Do you have a name?"

Name? What do I need a name for? All I am is a cluster of electrons.

"I've got to call you something. How about Cluster?"

Okay. If that makes you happy.

"I wonder what's next," you think.

The minefield of light.

"Mind your own business. I'm trying to think."

Go to PAGE 9.

"Time to go or get vaporized," warns Computer Control.

"I'm good and ready," you think to Cluster. "What should I do now?"

If you want to succeed in the minefield of light, set the controls for high speed.

If you decide to follow Cluster's high-speed advice, turn to PAGE 17.

If you decide to go slowly, go to PAGE 42.

You get ready to jump. *Maybe it isn't as far across as it looks,* you think. And so, backing up as far as you can, you leap out at the opposite cliff. The people all have their hands outstretched, ready to catch yours. And . . . they miss.

You're falling, falling, falling, falling into the deepest, darkest, most bottomless hole ever. After an unbelievably long time, you finally do hit a bottom, down in the dusty and dingy lower circuits of the machine. You don't mind the surroundings so much as the really dumb people — all video-game losers — you have to share your space with. Boy, are they stupid.

After a while all the dumb questions drive you crazy. For one thing, no one can do the simplest math problem, and no one ever remembers the right answers when you give them.

And so you get involved in conversations like: "We're having an argument. *He* says two plus two is five, but I say he's wrong. *I* say it's six."

And then you tell them the right answer.

"What did you say it was? Three?" It drives you cuckoo.

Still, it could be worse. Everyone down there *also* thinks you are a genius.

THE END

You hit the button, and faster than a speeding electron, you find yourself rocketing along, straight for a large black eye in the dinosaur's head. Before you know it, you've shot right through the eye and come out in some new dimension of the game world. Up ahead is an enormous landing strip where hundreds of spaceships like yours are lined up. The voice of Computer Control speaks:

"Welcome to the inner circuits. You are at the core of the game world. And now you have to play your way out."

Some other force takes over your controls, and gradually your ship settles down in the center of a circle of light. To your right and left are other circles. The door slides open and you step outside. And a human, a woman, steps from behind a ship and hisses at you: "Over here. Quickly!"

You can't believe it. Another human trapped in the game, too! You begin to move toward her.

At that moment a loud voice shouts out: "Attention, all game players. Return to your ships. Anyone caught outside a ship after the starting beep has sounded will become a starting beep himself."

What now? If you decide to follow the woman, turn to PAGE 7.

If you decide to go back to the ship, turn to PAGE 15.

The seven-headed dinosaur heads straight for you. Its middle head cocks back and wuzzah — a bright beam zooms toward you. You pull the control stick hard to the right. The beam misses but just barely. You feel the heat as it passes.

Gradually you guide your video ship around so you can keep an eye on the dinosaur. As you do, you notice two things: the big red FIRE button at the tip of your control stick and the bull's-eye pattern on the windshield. You can use it to line up your shots. The same head is getting ready to fire again. Carefully you line it up in your sights and press the FIRE button. In an instant, a fireball blasts out from the nose of your ship, hitting the dinosaur head right between the eyes.

Hey, this is pretty easy, you say to yourself. At the instant you think this, you feel a dinosaur death beam tear into your spaceship. Desperate, you grab the control stick and pull it to the left to get out of the way of another shot. Nothing happens. The dinosaur drifts in for the kill. You jiggle the stick like crazy, and the ship moves just enough to aim a shot.

What should you do — play dead until the dinosaur gets close enough for a sure kill? If that's your plan, go to PAGE 6.

Or should you go after it? If that's your plan, turn to PAGE 20.

Well, it looks as if the red wire is the one to try. You and the glitch take a deep breath. (Well, actually you're the only one who takes a deep breath. The glitch doesn't need to breathe.) Reaching down, you each grab the wire. The glitch nods an antenna, and with all the powers at your command, you direct your energies to your hands.

As you stand there, you notice it is having an effect. Your hands and then your arms and then the rest of you are disappearing. You picked the wrong wire, and a few seconds later, you are swooshing into the memory system of Computer Control.

It is sort of a dreary life, trapped in there with all those facts, but you can take some comfort in the fact that it would make your teachers very happy. Since you are directly connected to all the computer's brain-power, for the first time in your life you know all the answers.

THE END

It looks like a black-wire day, so with a little nervousness, you and the glitch grab the black wire, and as you are pulsing glitch power into it, hope for the best.

There is some sparking and flashing from the surface of the big, black board, and you and the glitch hear Computer Control's voice shout out one unmistakable word: "Huh?"

"We did it! We did it! We made it stupid," says the glitch, wiggling his antennae in excitement. "Come on, we'd better get going. It's only a matter of time before Computer Control repairs the damage."

With that, the two of you scramble toward the exit plug as fast as you can. You are almost there when two robotlike creatures with steel eyes step in front of you. Each is holding an electricity net, which they try to throw over you and the glitch.

They miss you but snare the glitch. You turn to help, but the glitch waves you back. "You get going. I've dealt with these deadheads before. Keep running!"

What should you do? One of the robots warns: "If you want to save your friend, you'd better stop where you are."

If you decide to go back, turn to PAGE 83.

If you decide to run for the exit, turn to PAGE 82.

You make a run for your ship, but before you reach it, Computer Control's voice comes on again: "Time is up!"

Every ship, including yours, takes off, leaving you stranded in the middle of this huge, empty landing area. Up above, you hear an odd crackling noise, and a powerful beam of light shoots down and surrounds you. In a matter of seconds, the blinding light is gone, and you find yourself in a huge, empty room with shimmering, white walls. One wall is inscribed with strange, glowing letters.

"WELCOME TO MAZEWORLD," it reads. "You are in the center of a multidimensional force field where things are not what they seem. Each section of the maze is a room without windows or doors. To get out you simply walk through a wall. Two surfaces in every room are electronic illusions. Depending on the route you choose, each step will either take you out of the maze or deeper into it."

You take a look around. Not even a doorknob in sight. You start touching walls. Your hand goes through the one on the right, and you also find that the wall opposite it is an illusion as well. It looks like there are two ways to go — left or right.

If you decide to go right, see PAGE 34.
If you decide to go left, go to PAGE 29.

Quickly you push the POWER SPONGE button, just before both dinosaurs blast you. The jolt rocks your ship, but a second later all the power comes back. It looks as if your power supply soaked up the energy from the death beams.

You decide to take advantage of this lucky break by leaning on your control stick, pushing it to FULL SPEED. The next thing you know, you've shot far away from the dimension of the Death-Beam Dinosaurs and crossed into a new game dimension. Off in the distance, you see specks of light, which turn out to be other video ships like yours.

Piloting the lead ship is a creature with a shiny metal face and two glowing dots for eyes. A message comes over your radio:

"Halt! You have trespassed into the realm of the Video Warriors. Unless you are prepared to do battle with us now, follow us and land where we instruct you."

Should you wait for these characters? If so, go to PAGE 46.

Or should you try to get away and go to PAGE 50?

Your eyes skim over the controls, looking for the high-speed setting.

Third lever from the end. Second row.

"Thanks, Cluster. Here we go. Hang on."

With what? I've got no arms.

"You'll think of something." Up ahead you see beams of red-and-green light piercing straight up through the gloom.

"What is this?" you think to Cluster.

The rules of the minefield of light state that you can fly through the green lights but not the red ones.

"Okay. Then we'll just steer for the green."

It's not that simple. The lights change color without warning and within milliseconds. If you happen to be in the middle of the wrong change — GOOD-BYE.

He barely gets this thought to you when you find yourself soaring straight into a large, green beam.

Left! Left! Cluster warns. You steer hard to the left just as the beam clicks to red.

Hang on. It'll change, Cluster reassures you. And sure enough it does, a split second before you hit it.

This is getting on your nerves. You are starting to doubt the wisdom of Cluster's advice to go so fast.

Should you slow down? If so, go to PAGE 42.

Or should you continue to speed on to PAGE 18?

You hit and hold the controls for high speed, but it's not easy. *Whiz! Zam!* There are more near misses than you want to count, and the palms of your hands get sweaty. But Cluster has picked a safe path, and after one last near miss, you skim out the other side, leaving the light beams far behind.

Time to head home, you decide. "How do we get out of this thing?" you think to Cluster.

I know a shortcut through one of the deep, dark circuits. Even Computer Control doesn't know about it.

"Want to bet?" says Computer Control. You don't know how the computer did it, but all of a sudden the rocket is gone, and you and Cluster are trapped inside some sort of energy container.

"Let us out of here," you demand. Computer Control ignores your plea.

"Now for a duel of the minds," Computer Control announces. "My great big, shiny mind against your puny little one. Since I made the challenge, you can pick who will set the rules for the challenge, you or me."

Be careful. If this seems like a trick, it probably is, Cluster thinks to you.

You decide to set the rules and go to PAGE 40.

You want to see what the computer has up its sleeve (if it had a sleeve), so turn to PAGE 43.

You agree to help, or at least listen to what the woman and her friends have planned. It turns out they want to distract the circuits by having a well-trained player challenge the computer to a game. While the computer is playing, the plan goes, they will try to find a weakness in the circuits.

"But why do you need me?" you ask.

"We have enough people to work on the circuits, but we need someone to play the games," explains the woman, who introduces herself as Philomena.

"But doesn't the computer know what you're trying to do?" you ask.

"Of course," says Philomena. "But it is convinced our plan is doomed to fail and just ignores us. I'll get our master strategist and have him explain the details to you."

She is barely out of your sight when one of the people standing around walks over.

"I saw you talking to Philomena," she says. "She's nice, but I wouldn't pay any attention to what she says. She's a little . . ." And the girl rolls her eyes and taps the side of her head with a fingertip. "My friends and I think we have already found a way out. If you want to join us, you're welcome. Just don't tell anyone else."

If you're suspicious and you prefer to wait for Philomena, turn to PAGE 48.

If you think it might pay to join the group, turn to PAGE 58.

You grab the video ship's speed control and shove it into overdrive. You bear down on the dinosaur one inch at a time. After what seems like years, the dinosaur fills your sights. You aim and fire a beam from your ship.

There is an enormous explosion! You and your ship drift right into the middle of the explosive cloud.

A voice comes on over your console: "Eject! Eject! Eject!" You see the bright red EJECT button on the control panel. You are about to press it when you hear another voice, Computer Control's: "You must eject to escape this game grid."

"Where do I go from here?"

"Nowhere. You've had your chance."

"What?" you shout back. "But I beat the dinosaur."

"True, but you were too sloppy. Your ship is a mess! I can't count that a victory."

"That isn't fair," you say. "It should be at least a draw. I did beat the thing."

"You have a point there, human. I'll tell you what. You eject from the ship, and I'll let you fight the dinosaurs another way."

Great, just great. Should you abandon your ship?

If you decide to eject and take on the dinosaurs again, turn to PAGE 67.

If you prefer to stay in the ship, turn to PAGE 27.

You don't trust the looks of the setup in the new rocket, so you jump away from the door as fast as you can. *I'm not going to be tricked again,* you decide. The strange, glowing creature gives you one last look, shuts the door, and zooms off. Now there is nothing else around. Nothing, that is, except one big green dinosaur.

And it's getting closer. Still no sign of any kind of help — another rocket, another anything — coming your way. Maybe you should have taken that ride. One of the dinosaur's heads cocks back. A sizzling death beam blasts out of its mouth, and just before you turn into a jumble cloud of overheated electrons, you have some last thoughts: *Maybe the ship will come back. Maybe this is all a joke. Maybe this is not*

THE END

Gradually the left head of the dinosaur slides into your sights. You fire and hit it. There is an enormous explosion that rocks your spaceship. By the time you lift your head you see . . . two dinosaurs.

You work every control lever you can find, but the best your little ship can do is to chug along at the pace of a sleepy snail. There is no way you can outrun these creatures. In fact, the beady-eyed dinosaurs are already circling for the kill. There is one on either side of you right now. What are they waiting for?

Computer Control comes over your cockpit speaker. "All right, human, this is your next-to-last chance."

"You mean this is not my last chance?"

"Don't be in such a hurry. I said your next-to-last chance. If you surrender now, your energies will be absorbed into my circuitry."

"And if I don't surrender?"

"Well, take a look around you." When you do, you see dinosaurs ready and waiting.

As your hand frantically skims over the controls, you see two buttons: one marked ULTRA POWER and the other marked POWER SPONGE. Maybe these will do something. Out of the corners of your eyes you see both dinosaurs getting ready to fire.

Go on to PAGE 23.

"Ready to surrender?" Computer Control asks.

"Give me a little more time. I'm still thinking," you say, trying to stall.

"Sure. You've got five seconds, and then the game starts, or shall we say, ends."

If you decide to hit ULTRA POWER, go to PAGE 11.

If you decide to hit the POWER SPONGE button, turn to PAGE 16.

You jump into the rocket and sit next to the glow-in-the-dark pilot. You try to talk to the strange character next to you.

"Hi."

The pilot looks straight ahead and says nothing. The rocket ship glides toward a gigantic arena bordered by walls of light. The ship lands in the middle of a metal field. Two figures walk up to you: a small, green version of the humanoid who piloted your ship, and a very tall, humanlike thing with some sort of metallic skin and two chrome ball bearings where its eyes should be.

"I have a message from Computer Control," the short figure announces. "The Master has decided to give you another chance."

"To do what?"

"To fight your way out of the computer by defeating the Video Gladiator. It's very simple. To win, all you have to do is tap the button on the creature's chest with this laser beam.

"Of course, the Gladiator will be armed as well," the man continues, "with this." And he pulls out a bigger and more dangerous-looking laser beam, which he hands to the creature with ball-bearing eyes.

Go on to PAGE 26.

A micromillisecond later, the Gladiator swings his laser and tries to slice off your head. You squat quickly and the beam whizzes by.

You jab at his side with your laser and sparks fly, but nothing else happens. He lunges again, but his beam goes by and hits the metal ground underneath. Looking up under his arm you can see a button. He moves his arm a little more and you see not one but two buttons. Which one are you supposed to hit: the red one or the green one?

If you decide to aim for the red one, turn to PAGE 55.

If you decide to hit the green one, turn to PAGE 64.

I'm going to stay with this ship, you think.

The instant you think this, Computer Control says: "So long, human. It was nice playing with you."

"I hope you short-circuit, you overgrown pocket calculator!" you shout back.

"Temper, temper."

Just about then, you realize that something strange happened when you blew up the dinosaur. You actually felt the video world around you shake from the explosion. Maybe that blast really shook up the computer. In fact, it also occurs to you that if the computer really had enough power, it would have absorbed you by now. Maybe it's too weak to do anything until it recharges. You might still be able to get away.

You decide to slip from the computer's grasp by flying the ship under the cover of the explosive cloud. You fly inside the cloud, but you are not sure which way to go.

If you decide to go right, turn to PAGE 35.

If you decide to head left, go to PAGE 45.

If you decide to go straight ahead, go on to PAGE 28.

28

Leaning hard on the speed control, you punch into the cloud and head straight ahead. You go a little too fast, so you have to pull back slightly on the ship's power. But it doesn't seem to matter, and you pick up even more speed. In another second you get through the explosive cloud.

"I made it! I made it!" you keep shouting.

"Not quite," says Computer Control.

"What do you mean? I survived the first game. Now I want out."

"It's not that simple, human. That game was just a warm-up. Now for the real fun."

"I don't want fun. I want out."

"You'll like this. Trust me."

"Do I have a choice?"

"Yes. You can trust me or be frazzled into a cloud of static electricity."

"I trust you," you say.

"That's better. Now we're going to move up to the next level of challenge. You should be honored. Not many get this far. You'd be surprised how many real klutzes we get in here."

"Okay. I'm honored, I'm honored. What do I have to do now?"

"We're going to have a little duel of the minds here—your brain against mine. You will have your choice of challenges.

To find out more about them, turn to PAGE 43.

As you lean to the left, the wall dissolves like smoke, and you walk straight through it. The bright light in the corridor hurts your eyes, and you have trouble focusing. By squinting a little, you can get a look at what's ahead. And it looks like what's ahead is nothing. Absolutely nothing.

The corridor curves to the left sharply, and although you are not sure, you have the sinking feeling that you are going around in one large circle, or heading toward a dead end. But you keep on walking just the same.

Finally you reach another wall, a solid one. You turn around to go back. In that split second, you notice the corridor has changed. What was one passageway has split into two.

So you are faced with two directions to go: either go down the brightly lit corridor on the left, or poke your way along the dim one on the right. Wait a minute! What's that on the floor? You can make out the faint, glowing outlines of two phantom footsteps. Out of curiosity, you place one foot on top of the first footprint. Immediately a whole trail of them appears ahead of you.

You follow them along until they take you to PAGE 47.

You run for it. "Watch out! Here comes a stray video blip!" Instinctively all the soldiers duck, and you make your move and head for the doorway.

You skip around the far side of the soldiers' ship just as a couple of them blast at you with their weapons. But rays bounce off their ship and knock them down. You hear their leader shout: "No blasting. We must take the human in one piece."

You zoom around the corner of the doorway, which connects to a hall humming with electrical wires. The footsteps of the soldiers rattle behind you, and you begin to think that maybe this wasn't such a hot idea after all.

One more sharp turn brings you to another long corridor and into what looks like a dead end. No time to go back. You can hear the soldiers getting closer. You press your back against the wall and hope the soldiers won't see you.

That's when you discover the wall is just a mirage. You can lean right through it. Some sort of tricky energy field, you guess. As you back away to study it, you find that you are walking through the opposite side of the corridor as well. Two fake walls—one on your right and one on your left. It looks as though you're trapped in some kind of maze.

Go on to PAGE 31.

As you wonder whether or not to investigate the fake walls, you hear one of the soldiers annnounce: "I've found the human!"

Not for long, you think. I think I'll do a disappearing act right about now. The only question is—through which wall?

If you decide to go through the one on the right, turn to PAGE 34.

If you decide to go through the one on the left, go to PAGE 29.

In just a few seconds, the WERM crawls out on the most exposed part of the wire. And that is when you decide to make your move.

As fast as you can, you lunge out from your hiding place and hit the WERM from behind. Absolutely nothing happens. It's as though the creature is glued to the spot. In fact, it is—by magnetic powers that let the creature walk where it wants.

And if that is not bad enough, the WERM lets out a high-pitched whine when you hit it. Right then you hear the sound of many, many other WERMs crawling through the computer in your direction. You can already see two coming toward you, and there are the sounds of many, many more on the way.

To someone outside the computer, it might look like just a quick flicker on the computer screen. Nothing special. Nothing to think twice about. But inside you know what caused that little flicker and flash. It was the moment when you went from being a human to a WERM snack.

THE END

You decide to go up, so getting down in a crouch, you try one powerful leap. To your amazement, you go bounding through the ceiling. In a matter of seconds you have jumped to another level of the maze. You look around and see no more maze corridors. All you can make out is an endless plain of shimmering light.

You are about to take a step when you hear the voice of Computer Control: "Congratulations! You have found the shortcut out of the maze. It is not often we get someone in here that lucky."

"Thanks. Now let me out of here."

"Why?" says Computer Control.

"Why? Why?" you shout. "You said I'd have to play my way out, and I did."

"I don't consider wandering through a maze a demonstration of skill. You still have to prove yourself."

"All right. But this time I get to choose the game to play."

After a few seconds of silence, Computer Control speaks: "Agreed. But it must be a game of skill."

"Of course."

"Well, I'm waiting. What's your game?" you are asked.

"Er. . . ." You stall around trying to think of something—anything you might be able to do better than a super-smart computer.

Please turn to PAGE 40.

You head right and step through the wall and into the beginning of another part of the mazelike passages. This is going to be a little tricky, you realize, because as soon as you stop walking, the whole room gets dark. Then, with each step, it lights up for a few seconds, and you can see what's ahead.

Then you get an idea. If each footstep turns on the light, why not keep it on by walking in place? You try it and it works. Now you can see corridors and walls up ahead. You walk up to one wall with your hand stretched out in front of you. The wall dissolves, and you step into another room. Touching all around, you find another fake wall on the left. And so you go on passing from one section into another and another and another. Before you know it, you are standing in a room with two doors.

Then Computer Control's voice comes on: "Attention, human. You are now in Room Nine, the next-to-last room of the maze. Behind each of these doors is a way out. Once opened, there is no going back. So choose carefully."

So you decide to open the door on the:

RIGHT because you have already had a few lucky right turns.   Open the door and go to PAGE 56.

LEFT because you think that is the last thing the computer would expect you to do. Open the door and turn to PAGE 70.

You swing the ship over to the right. Suddenly you notice the cloud is getting denser and blacker the farther you go. Also, you seem to be going more slowly, as though you are flying through a wall of Jell-O. Gradually you chug to a complete stop, and you are stuck in total blackness.

Then the voice of Computer Control comes on the speaker: "Funny you should head this way, human. It's saved me the trouble of chasing you down. I hope you're ready for the LAST game."

What, you wonder, *would that be?*

There is a loud *pong*, and the next thing you know, you have been reduced to a shimmering little video blip, part of a game of video tennis. And your sister Kate is having a lot of fun playing it. Unfortunately, Kate has a hot streak going today, so there you are bounding back and forth between two giant video tennis rackets in a forever game that you wish would

END

As soon as your foot touches the white square, you feel an odd, tingling sensation surging through your body. You look down at your feet and see them changing into something like a large pedestal. In a second or two you find out what that is. You have become a chess piece, a pawn.

"Not bad," says Computer Control. "Pretty soon I ought to have a complete set."

THE END

You hold your breath and step on the black square and nothing happens. You're safe. One good hop takes you over the next row of squares and onto the platform where the glowing capsule is. Without hesitating, you throw yourself into it. Inside are two small control levers. You grab each one and pull back just to see what happens.

The checkerboard room starts to fade away. Off in the distance you hear Computer Control shouting: "How about one more game? How about two out of three? How about . . ."

The next voice you hear is your sister's, who is pounding on the other side of your bedroom door. The controls you held in your hand are gone. A new Death-Beam Dinosaurs game is on the screen. "C'mon!" Kate is shouting. "Let me play just one game. Please? Please?"

You open the door and let her in. "Okay, Kate, Just one."

"Oh, boy, oh, boy," Kate says as she settles in front of the computer.

"You better play *really* well," you warn her.

"Yeah, yeah," she says. But you know she's not listening. She is staring at the small spaceship that has just appeared on the screen and is reaching out to touch it.

THE END

The Helper comes over and watches you work your number key. You get an odd number.

"Come with me. I'll take you to the odd game sector."

"Wait. I want to say good-bye to the others," you say.

"No time for that now. You can do it later." And so, without anyone noticing, you slip away with the Helper to play your game. He brings you to a large door. He takes your key, beams it at the lock, and opens the door to a large, black room. In the middle of it, on the floor, is a small, silvery object that looks a little like a flashlight.

"Here's your game room, and there is your game weapon," the Helper says. "Good luck," he adds with a peculiar smile. "You're going to need it." And with that, he seals shut the room.

You pick up the flashlight, and a bright light beams on overhead, projecting a pattern on the floor where you are standing. It's a bull's-eye, and you are at its dead center. There is something about all this that looks a little familiar.

All of a sudden there appear dozens of ugly, little creatures that look like some sort of hairy lumps with green, glowing eyes. They gather on the outer ring of the bull's-eye and are all starting to close in on you.

Go on to PAGE 39.

One comes a little too close. You point the flashlight gadget at one and press the button. A bright beam streams out of the flashlight/weapon, and the creature explodes in a flash.

You hear something behind you. You spin around, and there is another one of those things. You blast that one away. But there is another, and another, and another, and another and . . . all of a sudden you recognize the game that you're playing: The Last Stand in Space, the hardest video game of all. No one you know has ever made it to the end of the game without being gobbled up by these creatures, called the Mad Munchers. No one.

The Helper must have been the spy Philomena had warned you about earlier. It looks like the only one he was really there to help was Computer Control. It's only a matter of time before you become a bedtime snack for a bunch of Mad Munchers.

THE END

Hmm, you think. A joke contest might be just the thing. It's one area where computers are no match for people. No sense of humor. "How about a joke contest?" you ask. "The person, er . . . individual with the funniest joke wins."

"I don't know any jokes," says Computer Control.

"Oh, come on, you must have heard one or two in your lifetime. I tell you what. I'll start. What did the pocket calculator say to the math teacher?"

"I give up. What did it say?"

"You can count on me. Get it?"

"That's a joke?"

"I didn't say I knew any good jokes. It's your turn."

"All right. Why did the engineer use a four-eighty-eight interface on his mainframe?"

"I give up. Why?"

"To attach his peripherals."

"That stinks. That was worse than mine." You sense that the computer is really concentrating, and while it is thinking of a joke you notice the power cable running along the floor to the main circuits. *If I could get back into the circuit to the outside,* you think, *maybe I could get out.*

With that thought you grab the large cable and . . .

Go on to PAGE 41.

You grab hard, and for a second you see nothing because you are blinded by some kind of bright light. But once all the dazzle spots have cleared from your eyes, you find yourself right back where you were before, sitting in front of your computer. As you look at the screen, you notice it is frantic with all kinds of crazy activity. After a few seconds of that, the screen suddenly goes blank. Then, very slowly, seven words are spelled across it: WHY DID THE ROAD CROSS THE CHICKEN?

THE END

You move the controls into the first speed notch to move slowly.

Faster! Faster! thinks Cluster to you.

"Listen, I know what I'm do—" and a beam from the minefield comes ripping through the bottom of your craft.

All of a sudden you are not so sure about what you're doing. You decide to pick up speed, but it's too late. Another beam hits the side of the craft, bumping you off to the far reaches of the game zone. And as you drift, you find yourself floating somewhere near the surface of the video screen. You can actually look through the screen into your room. You see your mother step into the doorway and call your name.

You shout back, but of course she can't hear you. She looks around at the pile of empty boxes and all the electronic gear and shakes her head. "Sometimes I wonder about that child," she says aloud.

"I'm not a child!" you shout.

"What carelessness," she continues. "Look at this, the brand-new computer left sitting here still on." With that she reaches over to touch the power switch and by now her face is very close. You keep shouting, but it's no good. She can't hear you.

She turns the power OFF, forever sealing you in the computer.

THE END

"What kind of challenges do you have in mind?" you ask Computer Control.

"How about an amazing science-fact quiz in astronomy? I ask you three questions. You only have to get one correct to win."

"All right," you agree.

"First question: How much does the sun weigh?"

"What . . . ?"

"Time's up. The sun weighs 2.2 billion billion tons."

"Now wait a minute."

"A minute's too long. Next question: How often, on the average, is a new star born?"

"I don't know. About . . . "

"Time's up. A new star is born about every eighteen days.

"Last question: How old is the universe?"

"A trillion years . . ." you begin.

"Wrong. About eighteen billion years old. Too bad, you lost. But you do get my special prize."

A few microseconds later you find out what that is. The computer turns you into an energy pulse in its circuits. For the rest of your electronic life, every time someone types a question mark, you have to go to work.

Here's some warm-up practice for you: ????????????

THE END

You slap the coin down on your hand and uncover it slowly. Tails.

"Zone C it is, then," says Computer Control. "Pay attention now. Very shortly a bright C button will light up on your control panel. When it does, press it."

There is a soft whir, and just as promised, a lighted button flashes on. You press it hard. As you hold your finger there, the whir gets louder and louder. All around you the ship shudders and dissolves before your eyes. You have this creepy feeling that this is not going to be a pleasant trip.

"What is this Zone C?" you want to know.

A spooky mechanical laugh comes roaring out of your speaker. "I am Zone C. By pressing that button you have surrendered your intellectual power to me. And I can always use one more jolt from a new brain."

While all this is going on, the people in the laboratory down the street have found out about the mistaken delivery and come to your house to pick up the computer and bring it back to their laboratory. It seems to be in fine shape except for one thing. Every time a computer operator presses the C button on the keyboard, the screen lights up with one word: "Help!" No one can explain why this happens, but one of the scientists says he is confident he can wipe out that annoying message.

THE END

Quickly you swing your ship to the left. Just up ahead, through the haze, you make out what looks like an opening in the mist. You steer toward it. Lucky thing you decided to go this way.

The break in the mist veiled the entrance to a tunnel, and as soon as you approach it you feel a force take over the controls of your ship. As quickly as a frog swallows a fly, the tunnel gulps you down whole, and you race along its insides. A few seconds — or is it days? — later you shoot out the other end. You soar toward another giant video screen straight ahead. Just before you hit it, you realize what has happened.

You have been drawn into a game warp. Return to your first game on PAGE 5.

46

You decide to wait quietly while the warrior ships force you to land. You barely touch down when electronic soldiers scramble out of their ships and surround yours. Each has a little black box in his hand.

One of the soldiers calls you out of your ship. "Sorry," you say. "I can't come out today."

Hearing that, the leader gives a signal to the rest of the soldiers. They all press their little gadgets. Your ship disappears in a flash. "Okay, you convinced me."

Just then, a transparent rocket ship with a shimmering humanoid at the controls zooms up next to you. Its doors slide open. Their leader explains: "This ship will bring you to your next challenge."

"I'm ready for anything, as long as it's not hard," you say.

"It will be interesting," the leader continues, "as interesting as it was to the others who tried — and failed."

Sounds like trouble, you think. You wonder if there's any escape. The pilot motions to you to get into the rocket ship.

If you decide to run for it, turn to PAGE 30.

If you decide to meet the next challenge, turn to PAGE 25.

You follow the footprints down a dim corridor. A few twists and turns later, you walk straight into a wall. As you turn around to retrace your steps, you catch sight of a small gold plaque on the wall. There is some writing on it. You read. It's a riddle:

"You've reached the end of your
     short flight.
You can't go left. You can't go right.
You can't go forward or turn around.
Your only hope is up or down."

Great. You're stuck inside of a computer, and the only help you get is some dumb poem. You try the wall in front of you. Solid. You test the ones on the right and left. Both very solid. You turn around and walk smack into another wall, also very solid. Trapped.

Or are you? If your only hope is up or down . . . . You poke your hand right up through the ceiling as though there's nothing there. You stomp on the floor, and your foot goes partly through, as though you're stepping into a snowbank. It looks as if there really are two ways out.

If you're reading this section of the book in the morning, go down and turn to PAGE 93.

If you're reading it in the afternoon, go up and turn to PAGE 33.

You decide to stick around and see what Philomena does. After a short time, she returns with an old man. She describes him as the Wise Man of the Circuits.

The plan, says the Wise Man, is very simple. Since the innards of the computer are very delicate, a short circuit in the right place is all it would take to weaken it. "Are you willing to help?" he asks.

You say yes, and the group forms a human chain. The chain stretches out across a broad space. At the far end, Philomena tightly grips a bare computer chip mounted in the wall. When everyone is lined up, you notice a gigantic silver knob holding down several wires.

"All right, everyone stretch out," Philomena instructs. And when they do, she turns to you and says, "Grab that knob."

You reach out and barely touch the enormous connector when a jolt of electric power pulses through you, knocking you to the floor.

"Someone let go and broke the chain," Philomena complains. "Let's do that again."

What? Is she crazy? you think. *Do that again?*

If you decide it might be safer to try something else, turn to PAGE 59.

If you are willing to give it one more shot, see PAGE 61.

You decide to turn around and run for the wide open spaces, but that is when you find out your ship can only go in one direction — straight ahead. And that is where this group of weird-looking pilots is waiting. Gradually your ship shifts closer and closer to them. You wonder what they plan to do.

In a short time you have your answer. They all hit their ray guns at once, turning you and your ship into a bright little sparkle of light on the computer video screen.

"Hey, this is a great game," your little sister says, staring at the screen. "If I could only figure out how to make the computer replay that last scene. I'd like to blast that little ship again." Little does Kate know that in the world of video warfare you get only one chance before you meet your

END

You bring the Helper along as a guide. The Wise Man shakes your hand and wishes you luck.

You and the Helper set off on your quest, wandering between giant towers of electronic computer parts that soar above you like so many skyscrapers. Your eyes, however, are fixed on the red cable that will take you to the computer core. And the Helper's eyes are fixed on you.

After a short while, you realize that you're the one leading the way. He seems to be hanging back a little, perhaps looking for danger from behind. As you move through the gloom of the computer parts, you notice that the red cable turns sharply to the left. When you begin to turn that way, your guide steps up to you and whispers: "Not over there. Keep walking straight."

"But the cable is going to the left," you point out.

"The group forgot to tell you about the switchover here," he explains.

You hesitate. With a shrug, you pick up a trail by following a white cable that moves along a twisty path through the computer wiring. Even so, you manage to follow the cable without too much trouble. Eventually you end up at a giant cylinder around which the cable is wrapped. There is a slot in one side of the cylinder.

Go on to PAGE 52.

"You're here," the Helper says quietly. "Step inside."

"But where is the golden triangle?" you say, looking around.

"The powers will work better in this area."

"All right. But I wish you people would get your plans straight," you say, stepping inside the cylinder. You barely put your foot inside when you hear a creepy, mechanical laugh.

"Welcome to the absorption chamber, human," the Helper shrieks before he fades away.

Finally it dawns on you. "You're a computer spy!"

"My, my, how smart we are today," he says as he disappears completely. He was just an illusion, a three-dimensional, fake person planted in the group by Computer Control, just as Philomena warned you. As the absorption chamber starts humming around you, one thought keeps running through your mind. *I was trapped by a ghost. Trapped by a ghost. Trapped by a ghost. Trapped by . . .*"

THE END

You'll probably go faster traveling alone, you decide. So, after thanking the Helper for his offer, you search out the red cable and set off on the trail of the computer core.

As soon as you step away from the group, you begin to count. The plan is that by the time you count to one hundred, you should be standing in the golden triangle. When you reach the last number, you are to wait for the power to be beamed to you.

At the count of thirty, everything is going smoothly. You pull aside a heavy cluster of cables and pick up the track of the red one again.

Eventually the red cable leads to a clearing in the circuitry. And there on the floor, just as predicted, is the golden triangle. Still counting, you get up to seventy. In a few more seconds you will receive the beamed power. You position yourself in the triangle. By the time you count to one hundred, you actually do feel the surge of something running through you.

Out of the darkness, you hear the computer voice warning you: "Do not tamper with the core!" But you ignore the warnings.

A few minutes later the group finds you and gives you a big cheer. "It worked! It worked!" Philomena shouts. "Now is our chance to get free before the computer has time to repair itself. Form a power ring."

Go on to PAGE 54.

Everyone gathers in a circle and joins hands. Then, using their powers of concentration, they try to project themselves out of the computer. You feel a little dizzy and notice that some of the people are becoming transparent.

There is a moment of confusion. You're not sure what has happened, but suddenly it seems like the plan worked. You are no longer inside the computer. The only problem is you're not sure where you are. It looks like you and the rest of the group are all inside a giant warehouse. Looking out a window, you can see a high, wire fence and some guards and the roof of your house. It's the laboratory in your neighborhood!

You're so excited, you run around to all the computer people, shouting, "I'm back! I'm back home!" Then a door swings open, and standing there are a stone-faced man and two armed guards.

"I'm sorry," he says. "You cannot leave just yet. You see, that computer is a top-secret project, and we cannot take a chance on word of it leaking out. I'm afraid you'll have to stay here for a while until we think it is safe enough to tell the world about this. By the year 2050 I think it will be okay to let you go. In the meantime, we have a nice little top-secret hotel set up here with all the video games you could ever want!"

THE END

You thrust up and just manage to tap the red button with your laser. Something strange happens when you do. A glittering fog descends over you and the Gladiator, and you feel a little dizzy. You drop to your knees. The laser weapon drops from your hand. You can't think clearly.

Gradually the fog lifts, and when you look up, you see that your opponent has changed. It no longer has metallic skin and ball-bearing eyes. It looks like a human. In fact, it looks exactly like you.

Your "twin" picks up the laser beam and swings it at you. You fight back but make no progress. It's like fighting with your shadow. For every move you make, it makes an identical one.

You fight, but you know you will never beat your opponent. How could you when your opponent is you? For that reason, no one will ever win this battle, and you are doomed to battle in a fight without an

END

The door on the right swings open onto an enormous checkerboard. In the center is a capsule constructed of light beams.

"Hold it!" says a voice. A weird, glowing form steps right out of the wall next to you. It has arms and legs but no face—just a ball of light for a head.

"Who are you?" you ask.

"I am the Games Master. My job is to instruct you on this last challenge."

"It doesn't look all that hard to me."

"If you step on an improper square, you will become a spark in the microcircuitry."

"I'm doomed. Is that it?"

"Actually, no. Slip on this mental hologram band. It projects three thought images of you, which you can direct with your mind. They are your pathfinders and will walk ahead. If they step on a wrong square, they, not you, will dissolve."

"But what happens if all three get dissolved?"

"You had better be very, very lucky."

Three chances don't sound so bad. You put on the headband, and, amazingly, three shadowy figures that look just like you pop up. You send number one off on a black square and *piff*! It winks into nothingness. You send image number two onto a white square and all is calm. Nothing happens.

Go on to PAGE 57.

Carefully, you and image number three follow behind. But about three squares later, image number two's square comes up, and it also blinks into nothingness. That leaves you and number three. You decide to do a little sidestepping.

You send image number three one square to the side, and nothing happens. One more square forward. *Piff!* And that now leaves you all by yourself. There are two rows of squares between you and that capsule—too far to hop or jump. You have no choice. You will have to step on at least one more square. Black or white?

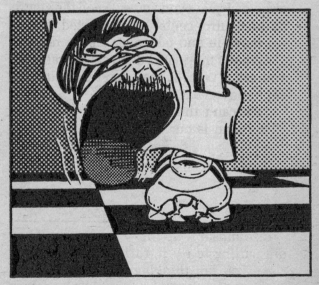

If you choose white, turn to PAGE 36.
If you pick black, go to PAGE 37.

Safety in numbers, you think, deciding to join the group. Their plan is to take control of the computer section in charge of letting things in and out of the machine.

"What can I do?" you ask.

"We need you as a sort of human sacrifice, a distraction for the guards," someone says.

"Sorry, I don't believe in human sacrifices, especially if I'm the main dish."

"Not a *real* sacrifice. We are just going to act as though we had captured you and drag you to the control center. Computer Control is very eager to get you in its circuits, as I guess you know. When the guards of the control center are distracted by you, we move in and take over the operation."

"What if the guards don't get distracted?" you ask. "What if they don't care that I'm captured? What if . . ."

"We can't think of that now," he says. "This plan is our only hope."

It sounds a little tricky to you, but if you are willing to try it, turn to PAGE 62.

As you are thinking this over, another group member comes up to you and says he has a better idea. If you decide to listen to that, turn to PAGE 68.

One shock is enough for you. "Look, I'm not going to grab that thing again," you protest. "I'm not ready to be turned into an extra-crispy human."

The others plead with you, but you refuse. No more chain-reaction short circuits. The Wise Man steps forward. "Perhaps this young person is right," he says. "There may well be a better way to defeat the circuits. We could join the group together and direct our combined thought power at the delicate core of the computer long enough to scramble its circuits and let the group break free. All that is needed is a person to stand near the main core sector and act as a sort of human antenna for all this thought.

"None of us can do that," continues the Wise Man, "because we have already been absorbed into the machine, and the computer can detect us coming. But you would be invisible to that detection system because Computer Control hasn't gotten you yet. Will you be our thought antenna?"

The first thing you want to know is if there will be any shocks. The Wise Man says no, so you agree.

Philomena and the Wise Man give you the directions. All you have to do is follow a certain red cable until it reaches a special gold triangle set in the computer floor.

Go on to PAGE 60.

"But it is very confusing getting there, and the human could get lost!" objects a distinguished-looking man, known as the Helper. "Let me go along to help the human find the way. I know the route well."

"No!" objects Philomena. "You are marked like the rest of us. We can't risk the computer picking up an unauthorized person near its critical area. It would ruin the plan."

"I will only go far enough to point the way," the Helper declares.

"Let the human decide if the Helper should go along," announces the Wise Man.

If you think you could use help finding your way, turn to PAGE 51.

If you think the plan might work better with you on your own, turn to PAGE 53.

Even though your head is numb and fuzzy from the jolt, you are willing to try the human short circuit just one more time. Struggling to your feet, you grab the hand of the person nearest you. This time you take a good long look down the line to make sure everyone is connected.

You take a deep breath and again reach out for that giant knob. Your fingers are shaking. You stop.

"I can't do it," you announce.

"Please. You've got to," the group begs. "It's our last chance." With all those faces staring at you, you can't refuse. You reach out again.

This time when you touch your target, there is a loud hum that quickly turns into a high-pitched squeal. Finally there is a loud pop, and all the lights go out in the room.

Gradually the light gets a little brighter, and you can see that you are standing in the middle of a familiar room—your bedroom. You made it! You're out!

And so are about twenty other people. You hear your mother call up the stairs, "Dinner's ready. I hope you're hungry. I made a lot of food, and I don't want any leftovers tonight."

You take a good look at the crowd of hungry-looking people standing around you. "Don't worry," you shout back.

THE END

The group gathers around you and marches you off toward the control center.

"Do we have much farther to go?" you ask the girl next to you.

"Not far," she answers. "You can feel the energy already."

You concentrate, and she is right. In a few more minutes you are marching around a corner and there is the control center—a large glass box set into the floor. It has several wires coming from each of its sides. All around it stand the guards, huge soldiers with steel skin and glittering electronic eyes. They look up sharply when your group appears.

"We have captured the human," the girl announces to them. The guards excitedly move forward to see.

Now, you figure, is the moment for the takeover. But nothing happens. The people around you simply step aside and let the guards come at you. Could it have all been a trick?

Maybe something will happen yet. If you decide to wait a little longer, turn to PAGE 65.

You might just be able to burst past the guards and kick loose all the wire connections to the giant computer chip. If you decide to try, turn to PAGE 66.

Stretching up as far as you can, you manage to hit the Gladiator's green button with your laser. Instantly the warrior stops moving and starts laughing—harder and harder—until his whole body is shaking. The green button must be some sort of electronic funny bone, you figure.

The Gladiator is laughing so hard that little bits and pieces begin to fall off him. Soon the Gladiator has laughed himself into a small pile of junk.

Just about this time, you spot some movement at the other end of the metal arena. A group of gladiators heads in your direction. You run the other way and see another crowd—real humans like you. They seem friendlier, so you head their way.

As you approach the humans, one of them holds out her hand. "Here. Join our circuit." The group gathers in a circle, and you are the last piece. As soon as you complete the circle of hands, the scenery around you starts to spin. When the spinning stops, you find you've been transported to another part of the computer. A woman, who introduces herself as Philomena, stares at you with wild eyes. She looks desperate. "We need your help," she says.

Turn to PAGE 48.

You wait a few more seconds, and in that short amount of time, the group rushes by the surprised guards to the spot where the control cube rests. Furiously they yank wires as fast as they can. There is one more wire left still connected, and the guards rush over to protect it.

Too late. The leader of the rebels pulls it free. You hold your breath and wait for the computer system to shut down. And nothing happens.

"It's a fake. We've been tricked," one of the rebels yells. By then the guards have surrounded them all, and the deep voice of Computer Control fills the air.

"Did you really think it was going to be that easy?" he asks.

"Thanks a lot, you guys," you mutter as the guards lead you off. "What happens next?" you ask one of the guards.

"What happens next," the guard says, "is that you will become just another computer drone."

"You mean I'm stuck here forever?" you say in disbelief.

The voice of Computer Control pipes up. "Forever is a strong word, human. Let's just say that you won't have to worry about that homework assignment due next Monday, or any Monday for the next few thousand years."

THE END

You manage to burst past the guards to the cube on the floor. You are just about to kick away the large cable connected to it, when you have the feeling that it is not a real computer cube at all but just a realistic 3-D image projected on the floor.

So you jump over the spot and keep on running as hard and as fast as you can. The guards are following closely behind. In a few seconds, you are well into the maze of the computer's circuitry. You can hear the guards no longer.

The guards are lost, you think. And a second later you realize: *And so am I!*

You stumble around for what seems like hours and finally come across—can it be?—another computer just like this one. A computer inside a computer!

You walk up to it and there on the screen is what used to be your favorite game, Death-Beam Dinosaurs. You remember how all this began when you just touched your finger on the screen like this and—oh, no!—it's happening all over again.

And, just as before, you hear a voice come over the control panel of your rocket ship. "You are now in a video world inside a video world. The games you play are for real and the stakes are high. One false move and you get sent inside video world number two. Good luck, human."

THE END

You press the big, red EJECT button. There is a loud *boom*, and you float free of the ship. As you drift through the blackness of computer space, you hear Computer Control: "Ready to start again?"

"Ready as I'll ever be."

"Fine. Here is your first dinosaur."

Kabonk! Sure enough, another Death-Beam Dinosaur pops up in the video space in front of you. But this time the game is different. Something is missing.

"Where is my new weapon?" you want to know.

"What new weapon?" says Computer Control. "You are only entitled to one, and you wrecked yours."

"But you said I'd have a second chance."

"I said I'd let you fight the dinosaurs again, but I didn't say with what."

"That's not fair," you shout.

"Too bad, human."

Fooled again. But wait! You see a small point of light gaining fast on the dinosaur and then passing it. It's another rocket ship coming your way. It swoops up next to you, and a door slides back. You are about to jump inside when you see a strange, glowing humanoid form at the controls.

If you decide to get in this mysterious rocket, turn to PAGE 25.

If you prefer to wait alone in space and take your chances, turn to PAGE 21.

68

One of the group, a distinguished-looking man called the Helper, comes forward with Philomena to explain the scheme. Anyone who plays computer games knows that they get harder as the player gets better. To trick the computer, the Helper suggests challenging the computer to a game and then playing dumb. That will help keep the computer occupied while the rest of the group tries to overpower the circuits and break free.

"Sounds pretty good," you admit. "Who's the poor slob that has to do this?"

Everyone is looking at you silently.

"Me? I'm not good at that kind of thing. I would blow it, believe me."

"There is no one else," says the Helper. "We have all played our games and lost."

Thinking over the proposition a little more, you decide to go along with it. At that, the Helper brings over a small pocket calculator with an antenna sticking out one end. This is your game key. You punch in three numbers to get a game assignment.

Take today's date and use that for the numbers. If it's May 12, 1985, you would tap in 5-12-85 (fifth month, twelfth day, eighty-fifth year).

Write down your numbers and add them up. If the sum comes out to be an even number, turn to PAGE 69.

If it comes out to be odd, go to PAGE 38.

Your number turns out to be an even number, and the Helper nods approvingly. "It is a good omen," he tells you. "The even-numbered games are particularly easy. Now, please step over . . ."

You are about to move when you hear a shriek that stops both you and the Helper in your tracks. "Stop!" Philomena is shouting at you. "Don't go with him." She has her usual wild-eyed look.

The Helper walks over to her. "Now, Phil, will you please calm down? You're much too worried. The human can handle the game." He turns to you. "We'd better get going. There's not much time."

Philomena ignores him and steps over to the wall where there are some controls. But before she can do anything, the Helper takes her gently by the arms and leads her away. "Press that large black button on the wall!" she shouts over her shoulder. "Press it before it's too late!"

"Leave that alone!" the Helper warns you.

Now you are genuinely confused. You don't know if one or both of them is crazy. You have to decide something pretty quickly.

If you decide to press the button, turn to PAGE 85.

If you decide to stay with the Helper, turn to PAGE 79.

Hoping to outwit Computer Control, you head toward the opening in a wall of electronic wiring. You are almost through it when you hear a cry.

"The human is leaving!" A whole crowd of people is looking at you. You start running as fast as you can for any cover you can find. In your rush, you stumble on a large bundle of wires coming up from the floor. You slip behind a nearby wall and watch as most of the crowd goes running by. As you sit there, trying to decide what your next move will be, you hear a voice.

"Hey, you!"

At first you don't see anything, but after looking a little harder, you spot something down on the floor. It looks like a giant spider, except that it has skinny wires for legs, a bundle of computer parts for a body, and two very thin electrical wires for antennae. The voice seems to be broadcast from its two antennae.

Go to PAGE 71.

"If you want to get out of here, follow me, human," the thing says.

"Not so fast," you say. "Who . . . er, what are you?"

"I'm a glitch. A sworn enemy of the computer. I just wander around in here scrambling computer commands, confusing the circuits — that sort of thing. If you want to get away from those crazy people, follow me."

"No, thanks, I've had enough help."

You move off into the gloom, heading in the opposite direction from the way the crowd ran. But a few more steps bring you to the edge of an enormous cliff. Apparently, you climbed to the top of some gigantic computer component, and the only way off is either to go back the way you came or try to jump over to the next tower. You feel as if you're standing on top of a cliff a million miles high; but with a good running jump you could probably make it across to the top of the other one. Suddenly you hear the footsteps of the crowd heading in your direction. You have no other way left to go — unless you go with that glitch.

Which would you rather try?

Jumping across to the next cliff? Then turn to PAGE 73.

Or heading back to the glitch to seek a new route out of here? In that case, turn to PAGE 74.

After a second's hesitation, you press the FIRE button. There is a flash, a satisfying sizzle, and the dinosaur's right head disappears.

"Congratulations, human. You won," says the voice of Computer Control.

"Thanks," you reply. "Now can I go home?"

"In due time. You are now ready to move on to your next plateau of game playing: Phase *A*."

"What's that?"

"A duel with three Death-Beam Dinosaurs."

"Forget it."

"Okay. Well, that brings you to either Phase *B* or Phase C. You have to choose one."

"How will I know which one to pick?"

"Do you have a metacosmic decision-making disk in your pocket?"

You check and see. "Nope. All I have is a quarter."

"That'll do. Take it out and flip it. If it comes up heads, you must go to Zone *B*. If it is tails, you have to set course for Zone C."

Take a coin and flip it. If you get heads, turn to PAGE 8.

If you get tails, go to PAGE 44.

You decide to jump to the other computer tower. Backing up a bit until you have enough space, you take a good running start and leap. A second or two later, you just barely land on the other side.

The voices of the people grow louder, and very soon a small crowd appears on the spot you just jumped from. They are waving and yelling at you. You can't make out every word, but it's obvious they want you to return. You move away from the edge of the cliff, but you don't get very far before you back into a solid wall made out of some hard black material. In groping around, your hand touches on some kind of lever up on the wall.

This must be a power switch, you think. You grab it with both hands. When the crowd sees you do this, they start yelling even louder. They're telling you to leave the lever alone. You pull it anyway.

And when you do, you wish you hadn't. The ledge you're standing on disappears into the side of the cliff. In a few seconds you'll have nothing to stand on. The crowd sees your predicament and starts begging you: "Jump! Jump! There's still time." They're leaning far over the edge with their arms outstretched.

It's time to jump to PAGE 10.

Or pull the switch again and go to PAGE 76.

"Come on, hurry up!" the glitch shouts as he scrambles through an opening in a mass of wires. "Just stick with me, and I'll get you out of here, if that's what you really want," the glitch says.

"Of course that's what I really want. Why would I want to hang around inside this dump?" you ask.

"I don't know. It's not such a bad place once you get used to it. It may be just wires to you, but it's home to me."

"Yeah, well, you're welcome to it," you say. "My idea of home is a little dif — "

The glitch holds up a feeler for silence. You listen, and you hear something slowly dragging itself in your direction. The very sound makes your skin crawl.

"Exit time," the glitch says.

"What is it?"

"A Wandering Electronic Random Masher. A WERM, one of Computer Control's killer patrols. Their job is to roam the circuitry looking for glitches and other unauthorized individuals."

"What do they do if they capture you?"

"Capture? They don't know the meaning of the word. They roast whatever they find. Now you, for one, would make a great WERM equivalent of a double order of fries. Let's get going."

Go on to PAGE 75.

You are about to run when the WERM stops dead and seems to turn in your direction. You hold your breath and wait. The WERM turns away again. Now, when you look around, the glitch is gone. *Hmmmm.* He must have taken the circuitry tunnel straight ahead. Or did he? Maybe he decided to get lost in the tangle of wires and cables off to one side. The dragging and scraping noise of the WERM is getting louder. You have to decide what to do quickly.

If you decide to go straight, turn to PAGE 77.

If you want to step into the jungle of wires, go to PAGE 78.

You pull on the switch as hard as you can, but nothing much happens. Actually, something has, only you are not aware of it. You have activated a new video game: Catch the Mountaineer. A little video figure hangs on the side of the cliff, and a group of tiny video rescuers with safety nets below run back and forth and try to catch the Mountaineer (you) before you smash to the ground. Your sister Kate is playing the game, controlling the rescuers. You hope she is good.

THE END

You step straight ahead, and before long you hear a little movement up ahead. You caught up to the glitch. Or so you think, until you take a few more steps.

Before you is a giant, slimy, steel caterpillar dragging its body in your direction. A WERM.

Then you hear a familiar voice behind you. "Hey, human. Where'd you go? I thought you were right behind me." And then there is a pause as he spots the WERM. "Oh, I see you brought along a friend."

You turn and run behind the glitch's spidery body into an alleyway between two dark towers of electronic components. As the two of you hide there in the shadows, you see the WERM slowly dragging its shiny body on by. It moves along the edge of a high wire overlooking a live electricity bank. Just then it occurs to you that you could run up behind it and, with one good push, send it toppling over the edge. But when you tell your plan to the glitch, it shakes an antenna in disagreement.

"Better to leave those things alone," he warns. "WERMs may look dumb, but they're dangerous."

Still, you think it may be worth a try.

So, if you want to give it a push, turn to PAGE 32.

Or should you tag along with the glitch to PAGE 84?

You decide to follow the glitch and see where you end up. You run into the jungle of wires, hanging like tropical vines from the top and sides of a tunnel. In a few minutes you reach an electronic clearing. The glitch is there, waiting.

"You know, things would go a lot easier for both of us if you were a glitch," he observes.

"Yeah, and it would be better if you were a pizza. I wouldn't feel as hungry as I do. But what's that got to do with anything?"

"I was just thinking that if you had some of my skills, we could really get on the computer's nerves, and maybe he'd be so sick and tired of you he'd let you go. I could give you temporary glitch powers. They're limited to one-time use."

"You can! Go ahead and glitchify me."

At that, the glitch lays its antennae on your shoulders. You feel a tingling. "Now, what do you want to do, give Computer Control a really hard time, or just cause some mischief and get out of here?"

If you want to give Computer Control some serious trouble, turn to PAGE 91.

Or if you want to stir up some minor mischief before you get out, turn to PAGE 80.

You decide to stay with the Helper. The man hands you a metal headband with a long, thin wire leading to a machine.

"What is this?" you want to know.

"It's a mindpower enhancer," he explains. "As the game gets harder, special game-playing skills from this machine will pulse into your brain. Put it on."

You slip it on. Suddenly you hear the voice of Computer Control inside your head.

"Congratulations, human, you have now joined the population of my game beings." You try to yank the headband off, but it won't budge. You look around for the Helper.

"He can't help you. In fact, he never could. He was just a figure conjured up by me. Now just sit back and relax while I make you an official citizen of the wonderful world of video games."

It doesn't take very long, and it is certainly a lot less painful than the dentist. All of a sudden there you are in the middle of the video game called The Attack of the Killer Cockroaches. You're the little human figure chased across the screen by the scurrying monster insects. Unfortunately for you, it becomes the most popular video game ever, and you spend most of your waking hours running from one roach motel to another.

THE END

You decide that maybe a little mischief is in order, and when you tell the glitch, he has one suggestion to make.

"I would love to get at Computer Control's Logic Center. I've always wanted to scramble his thoughts at least for a few seconds. And maybe in the time he is confused, you could slip out of here."

"Why haven't you done this before?"

"Until now, I haven't come across anyone craz—uh, adventurous enough to try it."

You are already having some doubts, but since this is your chance to break free, you don't want to pass it by. The glitch continues to scramble on until he eventually locates what he's been looking for: the Board of Supreme Logic, a high sheet of black metal with silver wires running all over its surface. Running into the base of it are two larger wires—one red and one black.

"Okay. What we're going to do is simple. All that is necessary is that each of us grabs hold of the black wire here, and when I nod my antennae, you concentrate all of the glitch force I gave you onto your hands. This will make scrambled eggs of the computer's thoughts for about twenty seconds. That will give you time to get to the exit sector over there," he says, pointing to a large plug receptacle. "Ready?"

Go on to PAGE 81.

"Okay. Now grab the red wire."

"Wait a minute. You said it was the black wire before."

"Hmmm. So I did. You know I'm not sure *which* wire it is, to tell you the truth."

"What would happen if we grab the wrong wire?"

"You become part of the memory system. Very messy experience they tell me. Now I'm all confused. Which one do you think we should grab?"

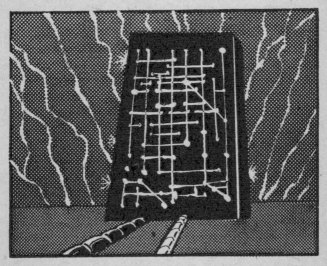

If you're reading this book on a Monday, Wednesday, Friday, or Sunday, grab the black wire and turn to PAGE 14.

If you're reading this on a Tuesday, Thursday, or Saturday, grab the red wire and turn to PAGE 13 to see what happens.

As you run toward the exit plug, you come to a long, dark passageway with a light at the end. You are running for what seems like days, when finally you get to the end— a wall of light.

Stepping closer, you see that it's actually a kind of waterfall of electrical current. And it is the way out of the computer.

But you don't know for sure if you can get through. As a test, you take off one of your shoes and throw it hard at the wall. There is a quick flash as it hits the wall, and it passes through to the other side.

Well, it's worth a try, you think. So, covering your face with your arms, you get a good running start and jump head first through the sparkling wall. Then you hit something with a crash. After you open your eyes, you see the walls of your bedroom.

Your younger sister is standing in the doorway staring at you strangely. "Where have you been? I've been looking all over for you. Where's your shoe?"

"It's a long story." You sigh.

And as you turn to your computer, you see a message printed on the screen: HAVE A NICE TRIP!—THE GLITCH.

"What's that on the screen? What's a glitch?" she asks.

"It's a long, l-o-n-g story," you say. "A long story."

THE END

Against the glitch's advice, you come back and face the two robots. "Okay. Let the glitch go. What do you want me to do?"

"We want to see what kind of a warrior you will make. Tricky people like you don't often end up in here, so we'd like to take the opportunity of trying you against one of our gladiators."

As they are talking, you notice that the glitch is quietly peeling away the net from its body and scampering off into the shadows on its skinny legs.

One robot turns to the other: "Erase the glitch, and then we'll take this human along with us."

"You were lying. You weren't going to let it go!" you say, trying to buy the glitch a little more getaway time.

"Of course we weren't. Why would we release our enemy?" And with that, the robots turn to find an empty net. "Well, you're not getting away. That's one thing we're sure of. Come on. It's time to meet the Video Warrior." And at that, one robot drags you over to a rocket ship with a glowing figure at the controls.

Turn to PAGE 25.

You decide to follow the glitch and head away. All those WERMs are starting to give you the creeps.

"I don't know exactly what you do," you say to the glitch.

"Well, let me give you a little demonstration." And with that, he scampers over to one of the many computer chips that pave the way ahead of you. "Okay. Now tell me something stupid you want to hear Computer Control say."

"I don't know. How about having it say glitch backward."

"Here goes." After studying the wiring for a few seconds, the glitch rests the tips of his antennae at two spots, and a small spark of electricity comes off them. About a second later, you hear Computer Control yelling: "Hctilg! Hctilg!"

"Pretty good, huh?" the glitch asks.

"Get that glitch!" you hear Computer Control bellow out.

"A little dangerous at times as well," the glitch adds. Just then, around the corner comes a huge WERM." Stay here. I know how to handle these tin crawlers."

So you stand and wait, but the glitch doesn't seem to be doing much of anything. The WERM is getting closer, and you are getting nervous.

Just the same, you decide to brave it out with the glitch on PAGE 86.

How much harm can there be in pressing one button, you wonder? And so you do. At that same moment the Helper disappears right in front of your eyes.

"Laser-generated illusion. A spy, courtesy of Computer Control," explains Philomena. "You just shut off the power that kept the Helper alive."

"You mean I killed him?"

"Actually it was more like you switched him off, like a light bulb. Hey, we'd better get going. I came to tell you that the group found a way out of here, and we're going to break free in a couple of minutes."

The two of you hurry off to join the others, and as you're scrambling along, Philomena continues to talk nonstop.

"You know, I've been sealed up inside this computer so long I've lost touch with what's been going on outside. One thing I'm looking forward to is a world where I'm not surrounded by computer games."

Should you tell her now, or let her find out for herself?

THE END

You wait patiently for the glitch to do something. Anything. But he just seems to be sitting there with his head down. You move toward him, not noticing the long wire on the floor. You trip and fall, right in front of the WERM.

It is merely inches away, when something like a steel wire fence appears out of nowhere between you and the WERM. You look up and see the glitch above you, hanging from one of the circuitry towers. He has spun something like a gigantic spider web. "An energy web," he tells you. "We've got to get going. It can only hold a WERM back for just so long."

"Thanks for saving me," you tell the glitch once you get free.

"That's okay. Anything to annoy Computer Control. That's my job."

By now you are starting to feel a little restless. You want to go home.

"Let's see what we can do about getting you out of here," the glitch says. "I think maybe we should start by getting into the central circuits of this gadget and seeing what we can do to it."

You suspect that maybe there is a simpler way. Besides, you got in here by yourself; you'd like to try and get out alone.

If that's your decision, go to PAGE 90.

If you want to hang out with the glitch, go to PAGE 88.

Together you and the glitch set off toward the central circuits to see what you can find. What you see when you get there is a group of all the trapped people who were ever drawn in by Computer Control. There were young video-game players, old players, good players, bad players, people who had underestimated the power of a computer.

After gathering them all together, the glitch announces his plan. He's going to gather everyone into a group to perform a superglitch such as the computer has never seen before. "We'll fry its circuits," he says.

With everyone lined up, the glitch goes down the long line of people and brushes each of them with his quivering antennae. The power of the glitch is now spread among them.

"Okay, now," the glitch instructs, "I want you to come together in a large ring, and at the count of three, use all your mental powers to fire an energy pulse into the core of the computer."

The group does as he says. Quietly they stand in the circle and wait for the glitch's command. On the count of three, they begin to concentrate. A little at a time, Computer Control begins to loosen its hold. Images of the people in the group waver and then begin to fade before your eyes. Then, in one last burst of sparks, they disappear.

Go on to PAGE 89.

"Hey, what do you know. It worked!" says the glitch.

"Great. But I have one queston."

"Shoot."

"When do I get out of here?"

"Holy smokes! I knew I forgot something. Listen, hang on to my antennae. I think I know a shortcut."

Still a little skeptical, you do as he says, and before you know it the glitch has taken off, and you're flying through the high-speed circuitry. The shortcut sends you ripping through the intense energy fields of Computer Control's memory banks. Finally the glitch sends you blasting straight out the screen in the front of the machine.

You shake your head to clear you vision and . . . there is your room. Somehow you feel different after having been dragged through the machine. And a few days later you find out why. You have absorbed some of the incredible memory power of the computer, and forever after you never forget anything ever said to you—a skill that never ceases to amaze your friends and dazzle your teachers. If you could only remember your name. Every time someone asks, you say: "It's Computer Control, human."

THE END

You set off down a separate line of circuits after thanking the glitch for its help. "Watch out for the WERMs!" he shouts in farewell. Not long after, you realize that you're hopelessly lost. It's dark, chilly, and lonely where you are, and even a grunting, creeping WERM would be a welcome sight at this point.

Parting some wire, you see a faint glow to your right off in the darkness. Stumbling over the computer innards and equipment in your path you finally reach the source of the glow: a giant door of some kind.

Cautiously you push the gleaming door open and see . . . what's on PAGE 56.

Revenge would be very sweet, you decide, so you tell the glitch you would like to get even with Computer Control before you escape. You decide that you'd like to cut off the computer's main source of nourishment: the electric power feed that goes to it.

The glitch is not so sure you have a good idea. "Electricity's tricky," he notes. "Others who have tried to shut down Computer Control this way had unfortunate accidents."

You tell the glitch you want to try it anyway, and so he leads you over to a pair of enormous wires.

The glitch shows you which wires are the main ones and then quietly steps away to watch. Under the glitch's distant guidance, and with all his power surging through you, you've just grabbed one wire when there is a blinding flash. You find yourself shooting through highways of electricity, out of the computer and right into the lines of current. You lose all track of where you're going. But in another instant, you discover that you have somehow shot into the wiring in your house, and a few seconds later you find that you are on television. Somehow your image got scrambled and mixed with your home television signal.

Go on to PAGE 92.

You can faintly hear your sister calling out, "Mom! Look who's on Saturday-morning cartoons." It's true. It is you, or at least a ghost image of you haunting your television set. At first they are upset to find one of the family locked inside the TV. But later they get used to it. You're the first in the family to have your own TV show.

THE END

Jumping very hard, you find that you can gradually make yourself sink down through the floor with each stomp. On the first stomp, you are down to your knees. Another stomp and you are down to your waist. With one more stomp, you punch through to the other side of the floor.

All at once everything gives way underneath you, and you are shooting down some kind of long slide. You're zooming faster and faster at breathtaking speeds. The grand windup seems to be a long, straight run right at what looks like a big steel wall. You tuck in your feet and cover your eyes, but at the last minute, the slide veers to the left. The next thing you know, you are skidding across the floor of a large room.

It looks vaguely familiar. On a distant wall you see a plaque, and as you walk toward it you start to read what it says: "WELCOME TO MAZEWORLD..." Oh, no! You're right back where you started. To get out, there are only two ways to go—through the fake wall on the left or the one on the right.

If you decide to go right, turn to PAGE 56.

If you decide to go left, go to PAGE 29.

Collect All Ten Twistaplot™ Books
And Choose From Over 200 Endings!

#1 The Time Raider by R.L. Stine
#2 The Train of Terror by Louise Munro Foley
#3 The Formula for Trouble by Megan Stine and H. William Stine
#4 Golden Sword of Dragonwalk by R.L. Stine
#5 The Sinister Studios of KESP-TV by Louise Munro Foley
#6 Crash Landing by Arthur Roth
#7 The Video Avenger by Douglas Colligan
#8 Race Into the Past by Megan Stine and H. William Stine
#9 Horrors of the Haunted Museum by R.L. Stine
#10 Mission of the Secret Spy Squad by Ruth Glick and Eileen Buckholtz